Poppa's Very Special Sunflower

Remember !
You are Special !
You have Purpose !

♡ Nonni
AKA *Linda Apple*

God Blessings Shown Cathy Mason

Written by Linda Apple

Illustrated by Cathy Gail Mason

www.lindaapple.com

Note to Parents and Educators

Dear Parents and Educators,

In today's society children are bombarded by media images and peer pressure, which, in turn, make them feel insecure about themselves. They feel the need to change themselves in order to be acceptable and as important as they perceive their peers.

There is an old saying, *bloom where you are planted*. I hope to convey this message in this story. We all are unique. No one is the same. That is what makes us special.

There are many springboards for discussion in this book:

- The meaning of purpose.
- Exploring the possibilities of our purpose.
- The folly of comparing ourselves to others.
- What it means to be content and grateful for who we are.
- Notice how the worm reflects the sunflower's moods. In the same way we can have that effect on those around us.
- No one can truly take credit for their physical beauty, but we can develop beauty in our souls.

I've also included mentor text to extrapolate additional teaching opportunities:

- How sunflowers follow the sun.
- The ecological importance of worms and bees.
- Find the ladybug on each page. Why are they called ladybugs?
- When the sunflower looks at the sun, notice that the worm is wearing sunglasses. It is never good to stare at the sun.
- The uniqueness of individuals. Consider our fingerprints and retinas!

It is my hope that all will enjoy this book and that it will provide many avenues for meaningful discussions.

Linda Apple

Dedication

I dedicate this book to my thirteen grandchildren, to my great-grandchildren yet to be born and to all generations after them.

I may not get to meet you on this earth, but I want you to know you were in Nonni's heart.

You all are special. You all have purpose.

Love,
Nonni

ISBN: 978-0-692-09874-5

Text copyright © 2018 by Linda Apple

Illustrations copyright © 2018 by Cathy Gail Mason

One spring day, Poppa planted three different kinds of sunflowers in three different patches.

His dog, Winston, chased butterflies.

1

After the seeds were planted, Poppa clapped the dirt off his hands.

"Winston, we are all done," he said.

But, when he knelt to tie his laces, he saw a tiny seed on his boot.

He laughed. "Well, I thought we were done."

Poppa planted the last seed. "Now we are done, Winston. Let's go eat lunch."

3

The tiny seed slept in the dark, moist earth.

A few days later, a warm, loving voice whispered, "Wake up my sleepy sunflowers."

Little Sunflower woke and pushed her roots deep into the soil.

Who had called to her?

She nudged her stem up, up, up, and popped her head through the soil

"Welcome to the garden, Little Sunflower!" said the voice.

"Who are you?" she asked.

The voice laughed. "Soon you will know. But, for now . . .

. . . you must grow."

And grow she did!

Each day she
grew taller and taller,

until . . .

. . .a tiny bud formed
on top of her stem!

When the petals hugging her bud unfolded, she
could see the garden all around her!

Butterflies
fluttered . . .

. . . and bees hummed their buzzy song.

8

"Hi there. My name is Sun."

"So, you are the warm voice," said Little Sunflower. "I am happy to meet you at last."

Little Sunflower loved the sun. Every morning she watched him rise in the east.

10

Day by day, she watched Sun travel across the sky . . .

. . .and sink below the horizon in the west every evening.

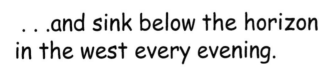

11

And when the moon rose into the starry night sky, Little Sunflower went to sleep happy.

12

One afternoon,
Little Sunflower
noticed the sunflowers
in the other patches
looked different from the
flowers in her patch.

In one patch, giant flowers grew, with big blooms on stems taller than Poppa.

14

In the other patch were flowers with
yellow petals ringed with red.

She stared at the plain, yellow flowers in her patch.

They were not tall.

They were not colorful.

They were just ordinary.

Who wanted to be ordinary? Certainly not her!

Little Sunflower decided to change herself. "I am going to make myself tall."

She lifted her face and leaves to the sky . . .

. . and stretched all morning . . .

. . .and all afternoon.

At the end of the day, she asked Neighbor Sunflower, "Do I look taller?"

He looked her up and down. "Nope."

When the moon rose into the starry night sky, Little Sunflower went to sleep sad.

19

The next morning she tried to change herself again.
She wanted be colorful. So, she closed her eyes and sang . . .

. . . *Orange and red*
and yellow and blue,
I want to be
colorful, too.

She sang all morning . . .

. . . and all afternoon.

Surely this would work.
It just *had* to.

20

At the end of the day, she turned to Neighbor Sunflower and asked, "What color am I?"

He smiled and said, "You are yellow."

"Yellow? No red or orange?"

"Nope," he said. "Just yellow."

When the moon rose into the starry night sky, Little Sunflower went to sleep sad.

Day after day, Sun moved across the sky, but Little Sunflower was too sad to watch.

Instead, she stared at the ground. Even though she knew Sun missed her, she didn't care.

She never wanted to look up again.

23

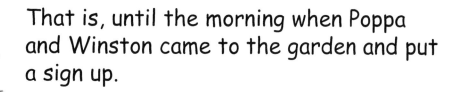

That is, until the morning when Poppa and Winston came to the garden and put a sign up.

"What are they doing?" she wondered.

Flowers
for sale
you Pick

Soon, people came to the patches and walked among the tall sunflowers, gathering them into their arms.

Others made beautiful bouquets
with the colorful ones.

When the people were gone, so were the flowers, except for the ones in her patch--the plain, ordinary, nothing-special flowers.

27

Why had Poppa planted the nothing-special flowers in the first place?

When Poppa returned to take down his sign, he asked, "How are my very special sunflowers?"

Little Sunflower frowned. "Special?"

Poppa put his finger under her bloom and lifted it. "Oh, you are the most special flowers in my garden. You have an important purpose."

"We do?" she replied.

"Yes," said Poppa. "Your seeds provide food for people and animals. That is your purpose and the reason I planted you. Besides, I think you are beautiful, too."

After Poppa left the garden, Little Sunflower turned to Neighbor Sunflower.

"Poppa said we are the most special flowers in the garden. We may not be tall or colorful, but that's okay. We have a different purpose— a very special purpose."

And when the moon rose into the starry night sky,
Little Sunflower went to sleep happy.

Linda Apple is the mother of five children and the grandmother of thirteen grandchildren. She lives with her husband, Neal, aka Poppa, and their Scotty dog, Winston, in Northwest Arkansas.

Cathy Mason is a teaching artist with the Arkansas Arts Council. Her art is displayed throughout the US and in Canada. She can be found online at www.cathymasonfineart.com.

Neal Apple, aka "Poppa."

Poppa

Winston

CPSIA information can be obtained
at www.ICGtesting.com
Printed in the USA
LVHW05n0603200418
574197LV00001BA/1/P